2nd-Grade
Friends

No More
Pumpkins

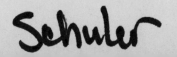

Schuler

2nd-Grade
Friends

No More
Pumpkins

2nd-Grade
Friends

No More
Pumpkins

Peter Catalanotto
and Pamela Schembri

SCHOLASTIC INC.
New York Toronto London Auckland Sydney
Mexico City New Delhi Hong Kong Buenos Aires

ISBN-13: 978-0-545-11352-6
ISBN-10: 0-545-11352-0

Text copyright © 2007 by Peter Catalanotto and Pamela Schembri.
Illustrations copyright © 2007 by Peter Catalanotto.
All rights reserved. Published by Scholastic Inc., 557 Broadway, New York, NY 10012,
by arrangement with Henry Holt and Company, LLC. SCHOLASTIC and associated
logos are trademarks and/or registered trademarks of Scholastic Inc.

12 11 10 9 8 7 6   10 11 12 13/0

Printed in the U.S.A.   23

First Scholastic printing, September 2008

Book designed by Amelia May Anderson and Véronique Lefèvre Sweet

To Aubrey Levy, Davide Mussari,
and Robert Trachtenberg, with gratitude for
the creativity you've inspired in Chelsea

—*P. C.*

To my mom, with love

—*P. S.*

Contents

Chapter 1

Mr. Marvin's Big Idea

Emily was tired of pumpkins.

In her second-grade class they had weighed pumpkins, measured pumpkins, and counted seeds from pumpkins.

They went to a pumpkin farm.

They tasted pumpkin bread, pumpkin pie, and pumpkin soup.

They heard pumpkin stories.

They wrote pumpkin poems.

Everything was pumpkin.

Pumpkin. Pumpkin. Pumpkin.

"I wish we could just carve jack-o'-lanterns," Emily said to her friend Vinni at recess.

"Yeah," said Vinni. "I can't wait. Mine's going to be a witch."

"Really?" asked Emily. "How will you do that?"

"I'll just draw it and cut it," said Vinni. "But I'm going to add a sparkly hat and earrings."

"Neat!" said Emily. "Maybe I'll make mine a cat."

Vinni jumped off her swing. "Hey! Tomorrow's your birthday party. Guess what I got you?"

"What?"

Vinni smiled. "A big, ripe pumpkin!"

Emily laughed and chased her inside the school building.

When they got back to class, their teacher Mr. Marvin had twenty-one pumpkins on the front table.

"*Now* what?" asked Vinni. She hung her coat in her cubby.

"Great," Emily said. "More pumpkins."

"Mr. Marvin!" Vinni called. "Did the pumpkin fairy visit us again?"

Mr. Marvin was not amused. "That's funny, Vincetta Louise. Sit down, everyone. This afternoon we are going to make jack-o'-lanterns."

"Yes!" the class cheered.

"But, we will *not* carve them."

The room went silent. Emily was confused. She scrunched her nose.

"Mr. Marvin," Vinni said, "you *have* to carve a jack-o'-lantern!"

"Vincetta Louise," Mr. Marvin said, "you *have* to raise your hand." He picked up a pumpkin. "Each of you will get *one* pumpkin. You can use paint, markers, yarn, glue, felt, beads, and buttons to make the pumpkin look"—Mr. Marvin was nodding— "like yourself." He had a huge grin on his face.

Emily had never seen Mr. Marvin
smile so big.
He looked just like a jack-o'-lantern.

Chapter 2

Pumpkin Portraits

The students pushed their desks together into groups of three. Emily sat with Vinni and Julia. Julia lived near Vinni. They rode the bus together.

"Before I hand out pumpkins," said Mr. Marvin, "I want you to write in your journals. Think of five descriptive words—"

"What's a descriptive word?" Vinni called out.

Mr. Marvin sighed. He looked at Vinni and raised his hand. Vinni slowly raised her hand and waited.

"Write five words to describe yourself," said Mr. Marvin. "Think of those words when you decorate your pumpkin."

Emily began immediately:

normel
frendly

good
reader

Vinni wrote:

cool
prety

Emily looked at Julia's journal. Julia had written:

pizza

dog

perpel

Emily said, "Um, Julia?"

"Hey!" said Vinni. "You're not a purple dog! Why did you write that?"

"Huh?" asked Julia. "These are things I really like!"

Emily and Vinni looked at each other.

"Oh," said Emily.

"Okay," said Vinni.

Mr. Marvin handed out the pumpkins.

Emily's was really tall.

Vinni's was short and fat.

Julia's was perfect.

"Hey, Julia," said Vinni. "How would you like to—?"

"*No trading!*" said Mr. Marvin.

"Rats," said Vinni. She looked at her journal. "Hey, I still need another word."

"How about SHOES?" asked Julia. She was writing GRAMPA.

Emily raised one eyebrow. She turned to Vinni, smiled, and asked, "What about BOSSY?"

"Yeah! That's a good one!" said Vinni. "How do you spell it?"

They decorated their pumpkins. Emily cut yarn for hair.

"This pumpkin would be a good head for Frankenstein," said Emily.

Vinni laughed. "Mine will look like Hamburger Head."

"My mom is bossy sometimes," said Julia.

Vinni looked at Emily.

Emily looked at Julia.

"My brother has a soccer game tomorrow." Julia turned to Emily. "So I can come to your birthday party for only two hours."

"That's okay," Emily said. "You'll still have time for cotton candy. And lots of rides on the golf cart."

"You might not get cake though," said Vinni.

"What kind of cake?" asked Julia.

"I don't know," said Emily. "But definitely *not* pumpkin."

Chapter 3

Moody Monday

On Monday morning Emily waited outside the school for Vinni and Julia.

"Where were *you*?" Emily asked Vinni. "Why weren't you at my party?"

"Isn't this hat really cool?" Vinni looked at herself in the glass door. "My Aunt Lisa bought it for me."

Emily glared at Vinni. She felt her face get hot. "*Well*?"

"Well, well, well," said Vinni. "The cat fell in the well."

Vinni marched off to the classroom.

"What cat?" asked Julia.

Emily ran to catch up. Julia followed. "Well?"

"Well *WHAT?*" asked Vinni.

"I called you three times," said Emily.

"I *wasn't* home! I had to go to my grandmother's."

"Why didn't you call me?"

"I was *at* my grandmother's!"

"Bet you didn't get glitter tattoos at your grandmother's," said Julia, "and all the cotton candy you could eat. I almost got sick when I—"

"*All right!*" said Vinni. "You told me a million times on the bus!" She jammed her coat and hat into her cubby and stomped to her seat.

"What is *she* so mad about?" Emily
asked Julia.

"I'd be mad if I missed your party,"
Julia said.

"Tomorrow night is Open House,"
said Mr. Marvin. "I've placed the
pumpkins on the back shelf."

Juan said, "I can hardly see them!"

"Please don't call out. I don't want anyone touching the pumpkins. I will bring them down this evening, when your parents come to school to meet me. Now, I want you to write a wonderful journal entry. Write about something exciting that you did. Yes"—he rubbed his hands together—"exciting."

Julia looked at Emily. "I'm going to write about your party."

Joey, at the next table, called, "Write about the golf cart!"

Emily laughed. "Yeah, when you crashed into the tree! The only tree in the whole yard!"

"Yeah!" said Joey. "Then backed up and hit it again."

"Write!" said Mr. Marvin. *"Don't talk."*

They began to write.

Julia whispered, "How do you spell MOONWALK?"

"Why?" asked Vinni. "Did you take a ride to the moon, too?"

"No," whispered Julia. "We had one of those bouncy houses. We jumped and did flips."

Vinni looked at Emily. "You had a Moonwalk at your party?"

Emily nodded. "It was really fun."

"Less talking, more writing!" said Mr. Marvin.

Vinni dug her pencil in the paper. The point snapped.

At lunch, Janelle said, "Emily, great party."

"Thanks," said Emily.

Vinni rolled her eyes.

At the water fountain, Juan smiled with fake fangs from his party bag.

Emily giggled.

Vinni snarled.

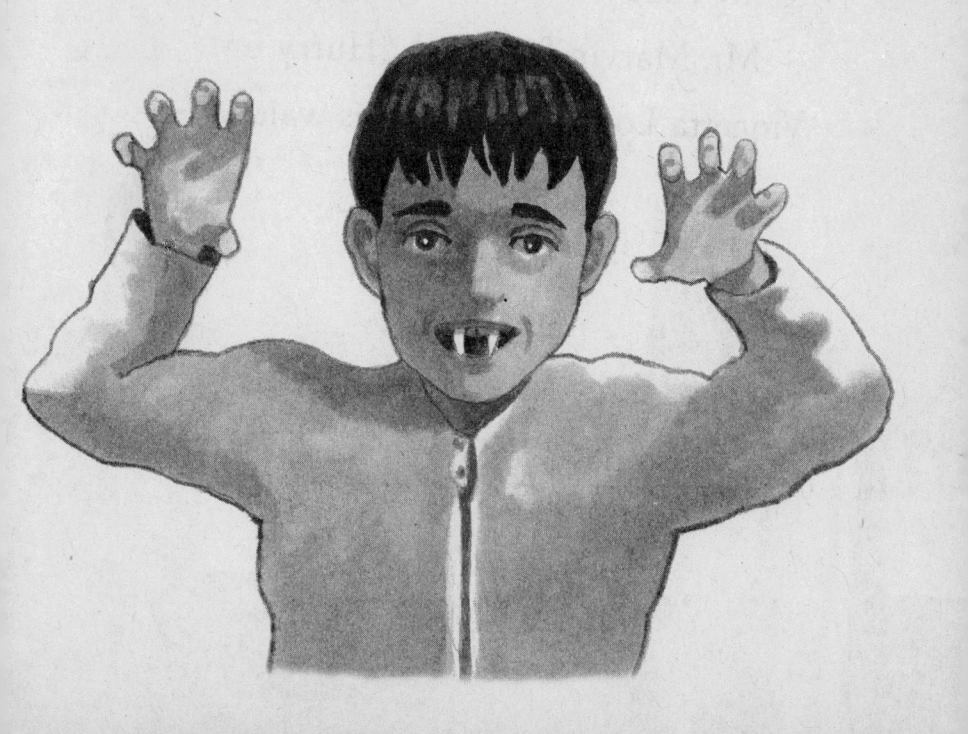

On the bus line to go home, Hannah said, "Emily, I wish tomorrow was Saturday, so we could have your birthday party all over again."

"Not me!" said Vinni. "I wish Saturday had never happened. I'm sick of it!" She turned to Mr. Marvin. "I need to go back to my cubby. I need to get my hat."

Mr. Marvin frowned. "Hurry up, Vincetta Louise. Your bus is waiting."

"Boy, what's her problem?" Hannah
asked.

Emily shrugged. She got on her
bus. Little Louie was in the front seat.
He wiped his nose on his sleeve.
Emily sat three seats behind him. She
looked out the window. Emily saw
Vinni run to her bus, but she didn't
see the sparkly hat.

Chapter 4

The Pumpkin Patch

The next morning Vinni did not look at Emily.

Emily did not speak to Vinni.

Mr. Marvin handed out index cards. "Print your name neatly on your card. Then place your card in front of your pumpkin."

Emily printed her name in fancy swirly letters.

"Vincetta Louise, is that *your* hand I see raised?" asked Mr. Marvin.

Vinni said, "I think I'm going to throw up."

"Quick!" said Mr. Marvin. "The nurse! Emily, you go with her."

Vinni froze.

Emily didn't move.

"Go! Now!"

In the hall Vinni stopped.

Emily asked, "Are you sick?"

Vinni didn't answer. She closed the
classroom door.

"What?" asked Emily.

Vinni crossed her arms tightly. She stared at the ground. "You remember yesterday . . . when everyone kept talking about your party?"

"Yes," said Emily.

"Remember how I didn't get to go . . .
because I had to go to my grandmother's?"
"Yes."

"Well . . . I kind of got mad. And . . .
remember when I went back to class . . .
after school . . . to get my hat?"

"Yes," said Emily. "But you didn't."

"Yeah, I know," said Vinni. "I . . . I . . .
well . . . just look at your pumpkin."

Emily peeked in the window.

Her mouth dropped open.

There was a hole in her pumpkin's
forehead.

"*Vinni!*" Emily yelled.

Vinni pulled her away from the door.

"Shhh!" Vinni started to cry.

Emily was furious. "Why did you *do* that?" she demanded.

"Shhh! Be quiet! I . . . I . . . I wanted to . . . I felt so . . . I was sick of . . ." Vinni flopped to the floor. She cried harder.

Emily stared at her. "Why?"

"Because . . . I missed your party. I
wanted to be at your party more than
anything else. But I couldn't. My mom
wouldn't let me. It just wasn't fair. So
when I went back to the classroom, I
stood on a chair, I took off my shoe—"

"And hit my pumpkin?" asked Emily.

"Yes," said Vinni, softly.

They were both quiet for several moments.

Finally, Emily said, "That wasn't very nice."

"I know," said Vinni.

"You should say you're sorry."

Vinni looked at Emily for the first time that day. "I *am* sorry. I'm so sorry, Emily."

Emily sat down next to Vinni. "I saved you some cotton candy," she said. She looked back to the classroom door. "Mr. Marvin's going to be mad. He wants everything to be perfect for Open House."

Vinni asked, "What are we going to do?"

"What are *you* going to do?" said Emily. "*You* ruined it."

Emily got up and walked to class. Vinni followed.

"All better, girls?" asked Mr. Marvin.

"Yes, much better," Vinni said. "But, Mr. Marvin, Joey's family portrait is hanging crooked outside. You should fix it before it falls."

"Oh, my goodness!" said Mr. Marvin. He hurried out into the hall.

Vinni grabbed her new sparkly hat from her cubby. She took Emily's pumpkin from the shelf and placed the hat on top of it. Emily wrinkled her nose.

"Just wait," Vinni said.

She took off her dangling earrings,
and stuck them in the sides of Emily's
pumpkin.

Emily smiled.

"Are you still mad?" asked Vinni.

"Well"—Emily put her arm around her best friend's shoulders—"you're just lucky I'm tired of pumpkins."